Storm

MW00511463

THE VERY BEST GIFT of ALL

John-Bryan Hopkins

Illustrated by
Drew Rose

SWEET
WATER
PRESS

The Very Best Gift of All
Copyright © 2005 by Sweetwater Press
Produced by Cliff Road Books

ISBN 1-58173-380-1

All rights reserved. With the exception of brief quotations in critical reviews or articles,
no part of this work may be reproduced or transmitted in any form or by any means,
electronic or mechanical, including photocopying, recording, or any information storage
and retrieval system, without permission in writing from the publisher.

Printed in China

This is the story of Mrs. Claus and her elves, and one very special elf in particular. His name is Terry.

Most people know that the elves at the North Pole make toys for Santa Claus. But did you know that Mrs. Claus is the one who takes care of the elves? She cooks for them, and sews their elf clothes, and tucks them into bed every night. And on Christmas, when all the work is done, she gives each elf a special gift.

One Christmas, Terry and his friends Merry and Berry and Perry had worked extra hard making the toys. Terry was proud of the way he put every wheel on every wagon just right. He made all the dolls pretty and all the toy

boats float. He made the teddy bears' eyes extra bright. He made the video games extra fun. He couldn't wait to see what Mrs. Claus would give him this year, because he had been extra extra good.

Together the elves helped Santa load the toys in his sleigh. "He'll never get off the ground!" said Merry. "Come on, if we all help, this will get done quicker!" said Terry. He noticed Mrs. Claus smiling at him and gave an extra push on Santa's sack. "Good work, elves!" said Mrs. Claus.

Santa took off into the night. Now it was that special time when the elves gathered around their Christmas tree to open their gifts from Mrs. Claus.

"I want a toy rocketship!" said Berry. "I want a ballerina that turns in three directions!" said Merry. "I want a super-size talking flying action figure!" said Perry. All the other elves chimed in.

Some wanted toys and some wanted clothes. Others wanted games and bicycles and skateboards. Terry sat quietly, knowing that Mrs. Claus had picked out something very special just for him.

The elves tore into their packages. Ribbons
and paper flew everywhere. Toys and games and
candy, sleds and skis and snowboards, paint sets and
rollerblades, coin collections and chemistry sets flashed

and sparkled as the elves opened
their gifts and showed them off.
Terry opened his box, holding
his breath. And out came...

A great big book. Terry didn't know what to think. It was just a book. Mrs. Claus had given him a book! Was that all? After all his hard work all year long? After he tried so hard to be good,

and not lose his temper (which he did sometimes)? Terry couldn't believe it. He looked around at all the sparkling gifts the other elves got, and a great big tear squeezed out of one eye.

Mrs. Claus was watching Terry. She could see him trying not to look sad and disappointed. Mrs. Claus picked up Terry and sat him down in her great big lap with his great big book. "Let's take a look at this together," she said.

Mrs. Claus turned to the first page of the book. It was a story about a boy who could fly. He wore a cape and took other children to a magic land where they saved everyone from pirates! Terry could see himself in that magic cape. He, too, would save the world from pirates!

The next story was about a brilliant detective who solved mysteries. The next was about a strong knight who fought a dragon. The next was about a brave explorer in outer space. Terry thought to himself, "I'm brilliant, strong, and brave, too!"

Terry was having so much fun reading his book, he forgot about the other elves. Merry was playing with her ballerina – until she twirled it one too many times and it broke.

Berry's toy rocketship
flew and flew – right out the window.

Perry's super-size action figure didn't work too well in the bath tub. In fact it rusted and stopped moving altogether. Terry finally looked up from his book when he heard Perry crying. "Perry, don't be sad," he said. "Come and read my book with me!"

That's when Perry and Merry and Berry, and all the other elves came over to see the wonderful magic book. They left the spilled chemistry sets and the bicycles with flat tires, the broken dolls and run-down video players on the floor. They spent the rest of Christmas reading stories. "This has been the best Christmas ever!" said Merry when they finished the book.

Terry only smiled. "I really did get the very best gift of all," he said quietly. All the elves nodded their heads. And they settled down to read Terry's book all over again.